BLACK HOLE RADIO KA'AZULA

ANN BIRDGENAW

ILLUSTRATIONS BY E.M. ROBERTS

DartFrog Plus

Printed in the United States of America

ISBN: 978-1-953910-52-3 (paperback)
ISBN: 978-1-953910-69-1 (ebook)

LCCN: 2022906374

DartFrog Plus

4697 Main Street
Manchester Center, VT 05255

I dedicate this book to the students of Solomon Schechter Academy—my amazing readers!

CONTENTS

HOME SWEET HOME-PLANET

can't run any faster, and I feel them bearing down on me. *Run!* I scream inside my head. Giant, robotic bugs are chasing me through the jungle, and they are closing in. I have to think fast. I jump over a thick bush and land with a tuck and roll. Turning over, I see them all leaping on top of me! Ants, roaches, bees, Ahhhhhhhh! I can't get away. My arms are heavy, and I can't move my legs.

"Whaaaaa . . . Huh? . . ." Looking around in a panic, I realize that it's my recurring nightmare. Again!

My heart is pounding, and I'm sweating, but relieved to find myself alone in my own room, in my own bed. Well, one tiny spider in the corner of the ceiling. But we have a deal: if the spider stays up there and leaves me alone, I will leave her alone. After our experience on Bilaluna, I have a new respect for insects.

I collapse onto my pillow. I should explain and tell you what happened to Matt, Celeste, and me on the second most unbelievable, intergalactic day of my life. I say the second because it has happened to us once before. Matt and I got sucked through the wormhole radio in the garage attached to our space club, where we were watching our favorite TV show, *Star Trekkers*. We ended up on planetoid Shnergla, whose aliens thought we were heroes coming to save them from some intergalactic bullies. Imagine *us heroes!* Then, our new friend Celeste had a cosmic conniption in our clubhouse and accidentally activated the wormhole radio again! We all landed on the moon Bilaluna and helped the cyborg alien insects save their dying world. They had a climate disaster that I hope we can avoid here on Earth. It's the second time that the radio has taken us to a planet that needed our help with a life or death situation.

You don't believe me, right? Yeah, sure, you're thinking, 'A portal to outer space in your garage! Intergalactic bullies and insect cyborgs! Ha!' Well, I have proof; Matt and I can read each other's minds with ESP. It's a gift we got from the Supreme Leader of Shnergla. It comes in handy for taming bullies and reading alien thoughts.

On planetoid Shnergla, I found out that my Grandpa had gone through the portal too when he was young. Bam! That blew my mind! Now I feel like everything we had ever done together prepared me to follow in his footsteps and continue the adventure. I don't think he meant for me to start so soon, but he died before he could tell me anything about it. I'm curious about what else is in those boxes of his stuff in the garage. The radio wormhole was wild enough, but I think he kept journals, and I feel like I'm ready to read them. It was tough for me when he died. I didn't know how to handle it. But I'm curious to learn more about his adventures and what messages he left for me.

I yawn and stretch and get out of bed, thinking about the question I want to ask Matt and Celeste today at school. Do they want to go through the radio wormhole again? Will they risk not being able to come back to home sweet home-planet Earth? Why? You ask. Is it worth the risk? Why do I feel some strange attraction to the cosmos? Gravitational pull, maybe? We were lucky the two planets we landed on were friendly and sent us back home. I could read his mind with our ESP if Matt were here, but he's not, so I'll let him tell you how this went down.

CHAPTER 1

MATT'S SLAM-DUNK

I can't stop thinking about the basketball tryouts last week. I really want to make the team this year! I try to concentrate on what Mom always says, 'Matt, you can accomplish whatever you set your mind to.'

When I meet up with Hawk at school, we go straight to the gym bulletin board to check the list of who got on the basketball team. Mom was right!

"Woohoo! I made the team!" I tell Hawk. I dance around him, dribbling an invisible ball.

"That's great, Matt!" he says, high-fiving me. Then we do our secret club handshake; we link fingers, do an interlocked fist pump, and click our NSA space-club rings together. "But look who else's name is on the list." Hawk and I look at each other and roll our eyes.

Big Mikey made the team too. He isn't fun to play with because he always hogs the ball and makes lousy shots. Mikey told me to try out for the basketball team because I'm half Black, so I wouldn't be half-bad at the game. "Yeah? Is that why you're so bad at basketball?" I shouted at him as he sauntered away, laughing with his buddies. I don't like saying things like that, but Pop told me I have to stand up for myself, especially when it comes to bullies. I'll show him; I've been practicing.

"Of course, Stretch O'Neal made the team," Hawk says, still checking out the list.

TRYOUT RESULTS
BAND
MATHLETICS

Stretch is our star player. He's always there for the rebound and scores as the ball bounces off the rim or backboard.

At practice, Coach Soggybottom tells me, "You made the team because of your defensive play, Matt. Keep up the good strategy!" And it's true—I had the most steals of anyone in the tryouts. I know when the player on the other side is going to pass the ball, and I jump in and intercept it many times a game. I am quick, but I also rely on intuition. Or is it ESP? Coach says Mikey made the team because he's good at gaining a position since he's so aggressive. "Yeah, no kidding," I say under my breath. Big Mikey is the school bully, and I've been avoiding him since Hawk and I fooled him using our ESP.

We're going to play our nemeses—the Bears from SSA Academy. They beat us by a ton last year in our first game. I see Hawk in the hall. "Hey dude, are you coming to see the Panthers take on the Bears today after school?" I ask him. "We need all the cheers we can get!"

"Yeah, sure, Matt! I'll see you there," he answers, hurrying into Mrs. Bupkiss' class. Hawk is so distracted these days. I think he's still a little down since his Grandpa died. He wants to find his Grandpa's diaries to read about his adventures in space. Unfortunately, they're in the same 'black hole' box with the radio. I'll help him look for the diaries, but I don't want to go near that radio ever again.

***

We've been playing great, and the game is tied with only 20 seconds left. The score is close because Stretch has been popping in all of Mikey's rebounds. But right now, we're doomed! Stretch fouled out of the game on the previous play. Their star player sinks his first foul shot, and they go up by one. Luckily, he misses his second foul shot, but without Stretch, the other team gets the rebound. They pass it around to stall for the rest of the game. I lunge for one of their passes. I can't intercept it, but I knock it away, and it goes right to Mikey. Even though Brad, one of our best shooters, is open, Mikey hogs the ball, as usual, and goes up the court himself. With only three seconds left on the clock, he throws up one of his lame shots. I crash the boards to try for the rebound. The other team's forwards are almost as tall as Stretch, so I'm sure I won't make it. Yet somehow, I slip through and get into a good position. I jump up as high as I can, noticing that Celeste is on her feet in the stands cheering me on. Mikey's shot is way too high and hits the backboard above the rim. Here's the weird part—I am airborne and catch the ball as it bounces off the backboard, then I slam-dunk the ball just as the buzzer goes off!

CHAPTER 2

WHOSE TRICK IS IT?

Scoring two points at the last second, we win by one. Pandemonium breaks out on the court and in the stands. My whole team is on their feet, amazed! I am shocked too. Before that moment, I couldn't jump high enough to touch the rim, let alone dunk the basketball!

Big Mikey runs up to me, all excited, "How did you do that, Matt? You're the hero of the game!" He high-fives me and runs off, leaving me standing there in a state of shock. Mikey just complimented *ME*!

After celebrating with the team, and when my coach's jaw is finally closed, Celeste and Hawk run over from the stands for high-fives all around.

Hawk yells, "Matt, you were flying; you must have jumped five feet in the air, man!"

"I never knew I could do that!" I answer, putting my hands on top of my afro.

Celeste opens her eyes wide and points at me. "Maybe that's the gift the Queen BEE talked about—you can levitate! There's no other explanation."

The Queen of Bilaluna promised one of us would have a gift—could it be telekinesis like their ANTs and FLYs have?

"I don't know," I reply slowly. "I never jumped that high in practice!" I continue, "and if I had that power, I'd be a much better shot—and the star of the team."

"Yeah," jokes Hawk, "your shots suck!"

"My final shot was great tonight," I say, strutting away, spinning the ball on the tip of my finger.

Celeste clears her throat. "Ahem! I have noticed that your shooting isn't the best. But how hard can it be?"

Not into sports and shy in front of crowds, Celeste looks around to make sure no one is watching. She grabs the ball from me and throws up a shot from half-court. Even though it's a sloppy shot, the ball falls dead through the center of the hoop—SWISH.

"Wow, beginner's luck," I exclaim.

"Oh yeah!" yells Celeste as she runs to the corner of the gym and throws up another three-pointer from the far baseline—SWISH.

"This game is easy," she shouts after sinking ten shots in a row from all over the court. We realize that it must be Celeste who got the gift of telekinesis from the Queen BEE.

"Maybe it's just a lucky ball," Hawk says, as he throws an air-ball that is way off target. "I guess not!" he says, chasing the ball.

"You got that right, dude," I say. "But how does Celeste's great shooting explain my slam-dunk?"

"When I saw you jumping for Mikey's rebound, I cheered hard for you to jump higher than the others and get the ball," says Celeste.

"Celeste must have levitated you," says Hawk with a chuckle.

I run and jump toward the rim and barely get half-way up. "Okay, I guess Celeste is the real hero of the game, and she didn't even know it. Haha."

"Celeste, you should join the team with your perfect shot!" says Hawk. "We'd never lose."

"Nah," answers Celeste, quickly looking away as she tucks a strand of red hair behind her ear. "It wouldn't be fair. And I wouldn't want all the attention."

Celeste is kind of shy and likes to keep a low profile. It has something to do with her autism. I don't care, I think she's cool and I'm glad she's my friend!

Walking out of the gym, I whisper to Celeste, "Can you come to all my games?"

CHAPTER 3

THE SHOOTING STAR

The next day, I see Celeste at her locker outside the classroom. "Hey Celeste, Coach Soggybottom wants to see you," I shout, trying to high-five her.

Celeste stops pulling her books out and looks at me with big eyes. "Why would he want to see me?" she says, ignoring my hand. I guess she's not as excited about it as I am.

"Well, you know how you were shooting the lights out after our last game? Your secret is out."

"What!? But, but . . . the gym was empty! Wasn't it?" she cries, darting her eyes around.

"No, the assistant coach, Mr. Stubs, was watching from the gallery. He saw you sink all those baskets."

" . . . and he wants me to play on the girls' team?" she reasons, pulling out her worry stone, rubbing it frantically.

"Nope, we don't have a girls' team."

"Oh no, he wants me to play with the boys?" Celeste's eyes go wider.

"I think so; he said you were just what we needed—a stellar outside shooter. Get it? 'Stellar'—Celeste." I laugh. "The jokes are writing themselves!" I try to high-five her again.

"Matt, this isn't funny. I don't want to be a star attraction on the boys' basketball team!" she cries, grabbing her stuff and taking off.

I chase after her. "You just have a talent, like other players have skills. And our team needs you, Celeste. We only won one game all last season."

"Well, if I play, I can't be the only scorer. I'll have to help you guys out too."

"Woohoo! You can help me out anytime! I'll jump so high, I can dunk alley-oop passes, and you can boost Stretch so he'll get even more rebounds." I start dancing around her, showing off my moves.

"Maybe I can help Big Mikey to pass more," she says.

"Good luck with that. But you could help Mouse out; he's always stuck on the bench. With a little help from you, he could be a great three-point shooter."

"Okay, okay! But I'm only going to help a little. Otherwise, it wouldn't be fair to the other teams. And don't tell anyone what I'm doing; they have to think it's all them," she says, rubbing her stone.

I laugh. "That's not a problem. No one would believe me anyway."

"Oh, and one other thing. I'll only play if Hawk plays too," she says, walking into class.

"Wait, that's going to be tricky. We'll have to convince coach he's good enough to play," I say, following her. "Why don't you bring him with you when you see the coach and help him sink a few. Make sure you both shoot the lights out!"

✳✳✳

After school, we all go to see Coach Soggybottom, and he asks Celeste to shoot a few baskets. She awkwardly picks up the basketball and dribbles it but accidentally kicks the ball away. She stops and looks at the gym floor, blushing. Hawk runs over to get it for her. He dribbles, passes it to Celeste, who catches it, dribbles it up to the three-point line, throws up a shot, and easily sinks it. I look at the coach and see he's scratching his chin. Hawk grabs the ball again, and this time he dribbles over to the right baseline as Celeste gets into position on the other side of the gym. He tosses the ball to her, and she throws another three-point shot and swishes it again. The next time Hawk passes to Celeste, she throws it back to him, and he tosses up a hook shot that banks perfectly off the backboard and goes swish into the basket. They keep doing this about twenty times until the coach says, "Ok, I want you both on the team! Be here tomorrow after school for practice."

CHAPTER 4

THE SOGGYBOTTOM TEAM

The next day, I tell Celeste and Hawk, "Coach Soggybottom wants you both to go straight to the gym and start shooting practice. He'll meet with the rest of the team to tell them you're joining us. Let's meet up after school."

Big Mikey comes up to me in the hallway. "Did you hear that Coach wants to have a team meeting before practice?" asks Mikey.

"Yeah, do you know what it's about?" I ask.

"Maybe he wants to congratulate us on our first win last game and give us all medals," guesses Mikey, smirking.

"Yeah, but probably without the 'medals' part," I sigh.

"I still can't believe how high you jumped on that buzzer shot. That was awesome!" says Mikey.

"Yeah, I can't believe it myself. But maybe we'll win more games if we start to believe in ourselves."

After school, in the locker room, Coach Soggybottom says, "Hi boys, glad you all came early. First, I wanted to congratulate you all on the win last week. Second, Assistant coach Stubs has something important to tell you."

"Thanks, Coach. Yes, great team effort last week. I watched it all from the gallery, and you guys played a great game. You moved well, and that finish was unbelievable. After everyone left the gym, Matt's friends, Hawk and Celeste, were playing a game of horse and daring each other to shoot from all over the court."

"Ha, do they even know what basketball is?" scoffs Mikey.

"Yes, they come to all our games," I jump in to defend them.

"Well, it appears so because Celeste never missed a shot. She scored from all over the court," says the coach.

"Maybe it was just a fluke; beginner's luck," snipes Mikey.

"No, she's the real deal. She shot the lights out in front of me too," states Coach Soggybottom. "And—I've asked her to join the team."

"But . . . but she's a girl! How can a girl play on a boys' team?" asks Brad.

"Yes, it's allowed and encouraged. Especially if there's no girls' team at the school," explains Assistant Stubs.

"Well, if it means I'll have some company on the bench, I'm all for it," pipes in Mouse.

"And, if it means I don't have to rebound every single shot—I vote yes too," adds Stretch.

"Well, it's not a vote. I've already decided Celeste will play. But I wanted to tell you before practice and ask you to be nice to her. With her amazing shooting, she'll really help the team. But she's very shy, and it's never easy for girls to play on a boys' team. I am counting on you all to be gentlemen," stresses Coach Soggybottom.

COACH
COACH

"Well, if she's that good, I'm all for it. And if anyone treats her badly, as captain, they'll have to answer to me," states Brad.

"Me too!" adds Stretch.

"And me three!" I pipe in, staring at Mikey.

"I don't know, a girl with red hair on our team," Mikey complains. Then, noticing we are all glaring at him, "What? It could be bad luck!"

Coach Soggybottom interrupts our argument, "Oh, and when she came to see me, she brought her friend Hawk. He didn't try out for the team, but he's got an amazing hook shot. He sunk ten in a row from outside the key," exclaims the Coach.

"Yeah, I've seen him do that in class, throwing garbage in the trash from across the room," I laugh.

"With the two of them, we'll have a full team. We'll have enough spares in case we get in foul trouble," explains Assistant Stubs.

"Okay, team, let's go meet our new teammates and have a great practice."

As we enter the gym, Celeste is at center court with a cart full of basketballs. She's shooting and swishing one after another into the basket at the far end. She doesn't notice us watching with her back to us, and she keeps shooting. Hawk is standing under the basket and catching the balls as they drop down from the net. He steps back, throws a hook shot at the basket on the sidewall of the gym, and every ball goes bonk off the backboard and swishes through the center of the basket. The whole team watches in wonder, mouths agape, as Celeste empties the cart—sixteen straight baskets, not one touching the rim. Hawk hooks each ball into the side basket, except for one that bounces off the rim and misses. If any of them had doubts, they are all convinced right then and there.

"Hey, nice hook shots, Hawk!" I say to drum up enthusiasm as Celeste and Hawk turn in surprise.

"And Celeste is a shooting star," exclaims Mouse, looking at her in awe.

CHAPTER 5

THE OTHER BIG QUESTION

The next day in UBSS Mission Control, we're having fun watching Celeste practice her super-power. She levitates eight small balls and revolves them around a volleyball to look like the planets in our solar system. What else would we do in the coolest space club *EVER*?

"My Very Educated Mother Just Served Us Noodles," she says, pointing at each of the balls in the air.

"Oh, good! Because I'm super hungry!" I joke, high-fiving Hawk and doing our space-club handshake.

"No, silly!" she groans, rolling her eyes. "It means Mercury, Venus, Earth, Mars, Jupiter, Saturn, Uranus, and Neptune. My dad, 'the astronomer,'" she says, making air quotes with her fingers, "taught me that trick to help me remember all of the planets in order from the Sun. It's called a mnemonic device, which helps you remember information."

Celeste is super-smart, and now that she has the gift of telekinesis, only she would create her own solar system.

"What about Pluto, Hawk? Why isn't Pluto a planet anymore?" I ask Hawk. He knows everything about outer space. That's why he's named after that famous dude, Stephen Hawking.

"Pluto was changed to dwarf planet in 2006 after discovering three other small planets the same size and orbit as Pluto's," he answers, sounding very scientific.

"Aw, that sucks! Pluto was my favorite planet and a cool name too!" I say. "It should be: My Very Educated Mother Just Served Us Nine Planets . . . not eight!" I keep my eyes on the tiny solar system Celeste is concentrating on spinning above us. "Hey, I just thought of something cool. Maybe your Grandpa went to Pluto!" I say, looking over at Hawk, who winces.

"I don't know. My Grandpa never told me about the radio or any of his wormhole travels. But now that I think of it, I believe he was preparing me to go on a trip with him," replies Hawk.

"Wow, sorry he died before he could do that," I reply sadly.

"How could he prepare you for that?" asks Celeste. "Gee, I wonder if he ever took your father on one of his trips?"

"I don't think he'd take my Dad. It's not really his thing. But Grandpa explained all about black holes, quasars, and wormholes to me. The last time I saw him before he died, he asked me to imagine what it would be like to travel through a wormhole."

"What did he say?" I ask.

"He said to remember what it felt like on the Spacey Mountain ride at *Wally World* and that you would be safe inside the hole. He said that's what he thought it would be like," sighs Hawk.

"Of course, he knew what it was like, and he was trying to prepare you so that you wouldn't be scared,"

Celeste says, keeping all her planets in perfect orbit around the sun.

Hawk starts choking on his cola and milk. "Whoa, I wonder if he helped any aliens like we did and whether he had any superpowers," he sputters.

"Yeah, maybe he could read minds or move objects around like this," Celeste says, looking up.

"Maybe he was the star of his basketball team. Sheesh, I really need to find those journals," Hawk starts to say when . . .

Beep, beep, beep, beep!

Four beeps and a pause coming from his garage.

All Celeste's balls fall from above and bounce around us as we stare at each other with our mouths open. The big ball bounces off my head, making my mouth snap shut. "Ouch!"

"I w-wa-was going to ask you if you want to go back through the wormhole, b-bu-but I th-th-think it's calling to us right n-n-n-now!" Hawk stammers.

Beep, beep, beep, beep! We hear it again.

I look around at Hawk and Celeste, whose eyes are as big as moons.

"I think it's time to go home, you guys!" says Celeste, getting up.

"Wait, Celeste!" Hawk jumps up and chases after her. "I was thinking that some other planet is calling us because they need our help!"

Hawk looks over at me to see my reaction, but I'm still rubbing my head and avoiding his eyes. I'm afraid of that radio.

"Matt, remember Shnergla, how we helped them

stand up to their bullies, and . . . and then we helped Bilaluna stop the destruction of their moon. Maybe someone else has a life-or-death problem, and we need to help them," Hawk pleads. "You've got to admit—we had some fun too; the air-scooters, RoACh-rides, and insect parades. Come on, you guys. Let's do it one more time. Then we'll think about how to close up the wormhole for good. What do you say?" he looks back and forth between us.

Beep, beep, beep, beep!

CHAPTER 6

WHOSE BIG IDEA?

"This better be worth it, Hawwwwkkk!" I yell as all three of us hold hands and spin like tops in zero gravity through a tunnel that seems to stretch and shrink, tilt and straighten as the cool flames snake by us at light speed. Then we mercifully slip into darkness.

I slowly open my eyes and look around. "Where are we?" A strong wind blows blue sand all around me, making everything appear blue; the ground, the sky, and everything in between.

I lift my head, which feels like it weighs ten tons. "Hawk, Celeste!" I call out, "Where are you guys?" I look around and spot them about 200 feet away, like two colorful sailboats on a blue ocean. *Am I hallucinating?*

I roll over and crawl towards them as they start to crawl towards me. I rub my eyes, trying to focus, but it's impossible with the wind and the sand. Suddenly the blueness in front of me seems to shift and move, and I realize that beings are approaching me—blue beings wearing blue military armor with blue ray guns! I hold up my hands in surrender, but the alien aims his gun at me and says, "Prepare for transport."

I feel a warm, tingly feeling from my toes up to my head, then a scary sensation that I am melting. Everything starts to swirl around me as I see the planet blur out and dissolve. I think I pass out for a second. When I open my eyes, I know that I've teleported to a hovering space-craft, and Hawk and Celeste are smiling at me!

"Dude, we were 'Beamed Up.'" Hawk cries. "Just like the Star Trekkers!" He tries to high-five me, but I am too weak to lift my arm. I watch as Hawk and Celeste high-five and talk excitedly to each other. They must have gotten here way before me.

"Matt, Matt!" I hear my name as if from far away. "Wake up! You've got to see this. This place is cool," Hawk says, shaking me. On the other side, Celeste is checking out the real live alien spaceship.

"Hey, guys, look at me!" she says, trying on a mask that makes her look like something from a horror movie.

"Yikes! Celeste, take that off. It gives me the creeps," I beg. It's a cross between a giant spider and a reptile with quills and dreadlocks hanging down. That woke me up! I get up to explore the navigation console with Hawk. Everything is clear plastic so that you can see the inner workings. With system status screens, back-lit panel displays are lit up in multiple colors. Toggle switches, gauges, and instruments blink randomly. "This is so cool!" I say, blown away by things I'd only seen in my favorite TV show.

"I could fly this thing. Yippee-Ki-Yay!" Hawk shouts, pretending to be the pilot on 'Star Trekkers.'

There are mumblings and snorts of alien conver-sation coming from a backroom. "What should we . . . these creatures . . . we can't trust them . . . we will bring them to TopMost . . ."

"Hey guys, we may be in trouble here," I warn them. "The aliens think we're dangerous."

"Dangerous? Maybe I shouldn't have eaten the candy he gave me," Hawk says.

"What candy, Hawk?" I ask. Now I'm interested.

"A blue candy, it was very tasty!" He opens his mouth to show us his blue tongue.

"Ooohhh gross!" says Celeste, making a face. "Hawk, you shouldn't have eaten some random, alien candy."

She walks over to get a closer look, noticing that more than Hawk's tongue is blue. His lips and face are also turning blue!

"What the . . . ? Ummmm, Hawk, you're starting to look like a blueberry," I say, noticing his skin is turning a dark blue color. Even his blond hair is going blue!

"Didn't your parents ever warn you not to take candy from strangers?" Celeste says, getting serious.

I turn because the blue aliens have emerged from the back room. They are taller than us and have two short arms ending in claws. Their muscular legs have talons with two long toes in front and one at the back like large birds! One of them holds out a blue 'candy' to me in his curved claw.

"No thanks!" I say, holding up my hand in a stop signal.

The two aliens look at each other with their enormous black eyes, long, sloping foreheads, and heavy brows furrowed. With my ESP, I understand their conversation. "What will we do if he will not take the sameness capsule?" one says. "TopMost will be very angry," the other answers. "Yes, we must insist," the first replies.

"Who's TopMost?" I ESP them.

Both aliens look around, confused. "Who spoke?" they ask each other, wriggling their blue-bird-like beaks and tiny horns on the side of their heads. I hold up a finger to indicate it was me.

"Who's TopMost, and why do I need to eat that?" I say, pointing at the pill.

They back away from me and run to the other room. I look over at Celeste's face to see she's turning blue also. "Celeste!" I say, walking towards her. "Did you eat the blue pill, too?"

"Ummm. I'm not sure. I came to, and they gave me water to drink, so I drank it! Why? What's happening???" she says, running over to a screen where she sees her reflection. "Oh no!" Celeste says with a sob, "I look like a Smurf! I can't go back to school looking like this!" she cries, trying to rub it off. "The girls will never be friends with me now!"

"It's okay, Celeste. The blue matches your eyes!" I say, trying to cheer her up. Celeste has trouble fitting in with the cool girls in the class.

"This is no joke, Matt. Look at us!" she cries, pointing from Hawk's blue face to her own. The only difference is that Celeste's red hair has stayed red.

That's when the blue aliens come back into the room with a syringe full of blue liquid, and they are walking in my direction.

CHAPTER 7

WE'VE GOT THE BLUES

I have never been so scared in my life! I back away, keeping my eyes on the needle threatening to enter my body.

"Wait a second, fellas." I hold out my hands, and they immediately grab hold of my wrists with their talons to inject the contents of the syringe. I know that needles are dangerous because my mom warned me never to touch them if I see them on the ground. Mom is a nurse, and she's always real careful with them.

"Noooooo!" I scream so loud inside my head that everyone stops for a split second. The blue beings freeze, just long enough for something amazing to happen! The syringe flies out of their grasp and smashes against the spaceship wall. Blue liquid oozes down the wall, and I breathe a sigh of relief.

The blue aliens' huge, black eyes almost bulge out of their heads as they run from the room again, snorting and sputtering to each other, totally freaked out.

"Whew! Thanks, Celeste! You saved my butt again with your super-power," I say, rubbing my wrists.

"Yeah, Celeste, you got them good with that move!" says Hawk in awe, looking bluer than ever.

"I couldn't let them inject you with that blue stuff too, so I wished the syringe away!" she says casually, looking at her reflection again. It always surprises me that Celeste is so relaxed about some things and yet so nervous about other little things. Like right now, she's totally casual about fending off two large alien beings for me.

"Celeste, maybe they'll trust us if we're blue like them?" Hawk replies.

"You think they'll want to hang out with us just because we have the same color skin? That's messed up." I say, slapping my forehead.

"I'm just saying that we'll fit in better. Like that episode of *Star Trekkers* where everyone had to stretch their ears and talk like robots to fool the Vulcans." Laughs Hawk. "Besides, it'll probably just wear off."

"But what if it doesn't?" Celeste cries, looking more like 'Smurfette in Space' every minute.

It's a good question, but we don't have time to deal with it right now as we hear the grunting and snorting of aliens arguing in the next room. They re-emerge and roughly lead us to the back wall of the ship and strap us against it. Right now, we have to figure out how to deal with these hostile aliens. At least Hawk and I can understand their thoughts with ESP.

"Snort! We will bring them in, and it will no longer be our problem," they mutter and grunt, walking to the front of the ship.

Suddenly the spacecraft bursts into life, and we are thrown back against the wall with such force that we can't move or talk . . . or hardly breathe. I think they are in a hurry to be free of us.

It is a short trip on the hyperspace highway. In a blink, I see my young life pass before my eyes— Hawk and I in preschool playing with our toy spaceships, my pop pushing me on the swings at the park, my mom making my favorite chocolate chip cookies . . . Yuummm! I can almost smell the chocolatey goodness. Whoosh! Trillions of stars streak by, casting an eerie glow in the mostly empty ship. I feel scared and worried. I have the creepy sensation that I may be a grown-up by the time we get there! I glance over at Hawk and Celeste to see that they are still blue ten-year-olds. Whew! That's good, I guess.

I have a panic attack as they carry us off the spaceship. The aliens separate us and take Hawk and Celeste to the right and me to the left. "Wait!" I whimper, but my captors ignore me and march me into their bubble world strapped to a stretcher. Above me, I see an outer shell made of thousands of solar panels. It looks like a power-generating megastructure. It's so futuristic—I think I've been transported thousands of years into the future. There's stuff happening all around me—blue aliens are coming and going, some grunting and chattering, and I notice their surprised reactions to my presence. Or maybe it's the color of my skin that is causing all the commotion? I've never had to worry so much about my skin color. My mom says my skin glitters like gold, but really it's just a bronze color. I feel guilty sometimes when my classmates think of me as white, but I don't correct them. Or, like if someone tells a joke about a black person, and I laugh along or don't say anything. Does that mean I'm a racist, too?

They unstrap me from the stretcher and leave me in a locked chamber, alone with my thoughts. I sit down, feeling sorry for myself. What have I gotten myself into? I hold my head in my hands. Now I'm in jail. My pop told me that, when he was a young protestor, he and his friends were put in jail because of the color of their skin. *Aarrgh!* I don't want to think about this stuff anymore. I start to cry. I just want to go back to my neighborhood on Earth where I can play basketball and video games without worrying about the color of my skin.

Rubbing my eyes, I notice a pile of blankets and rags in the corner and decide to investigate. I approach cautiously and reach out to pull a layer back when—something moves! I jump back and use my ESP, "Hello? Is there anybody in there?"

I am shocked to see a small red alien pop his head out of the pile and look around, confused. When he sees me, he immediately dives back undercover. I see the blankets shaking as he trembles under them.

"Hey, little dude, it's okay. My name is Matt, and I'm from Planet Earth." I slowly approach the quivering pile and pull the blanket back.

"You from other world?" a little voice says in my head as a small red face with a tiny beak and little horns looks shyly at me. He looks like the blue guys, but smaller—and bright red like Darth Maul, but way cuter.

"Yes. There are three of us, but your blue guys aren't too friendly," I say, pacing around the small room like a caged animal.

"Your cells are toxic; that is why you in disease chamber . . . with me," the little alien replies sadly, burrowing into the filthy rags again.

"You mean they think we have a disease because of the color of our skin?" I say, trying to understand. "Can you help me get out of here?" I ESP him.

"I cannot help even myself!" he cries miserably, trembling under the blanket.

"Maybe we can help each other?" I ask.

His head pops out, and he looks at me with a rag comically covering half his face. "No one offer Teal help before."

"Is that your name, little dude? Teal?" I ask, smiling, and he nods.

"Let's make a deal. If you help me get out of here, I'll help you get back to your family."

CHAPTER 8

THE GREAT ESCAPE

walk back towards the door. "Door locked," Teal says. "Will unlock only when bring worms. Eat time."

"They give you worms to eat?!" I cry, horrified.

"Yes, toxic ones get what food left. Have many worms on Ka'Azula," he says, sticking out his bird tongue and twitching his little red beak.

"That sucks," I say, knowing they'll give me worms to eat too. *We HAVE to get out of here!*

I stand at the door listening hard with ESP for clues. I hear muffled sounds coming from far away but getting closer.

"Okay, Teal, this is the plan. I'll hide behind the door. When the door opens, you distract the blue guy by screaming and pointing to the back of the room. I'll come out and throw the blanket over his head and push him into the wall. We'll run out the door and lock it behind us. Quick, I hear someone coming! Get ready!"

I grab a blanket and get in place. I look at Teal and wink. The door opens, and the blue guard slowly enters the chamber. I point at Teal, and he starts screaming at the top of his lungs and motioning toward the corner of the room. The surprised guard rushes in, looking around as I jump out with the blanket and cover his head with it. I push him into the wall, and he falls down, stunned.

"Come on, little dude! This is our chance! Run!" I grab his tiny claw and yank him to his feet as we run out the door, slamming it behind us. Breathing heavily, we look both ways, and I look at Teal for a sign of where to go. He points to the right, and we bolt down the corridor before anyone else comes out.

"Where's the exit?" I ESP, looking over my shoulder. I see someone blue in the distance, and I pull Teal into a doorway. I push on the door with both hands, not knowing how to open it. I look and feel all around for a knob or handle when Teal touches a side panel and two doors slide open from the middle. "Thanks," I say, smiling at him. We carefully enter, looking around for blue beings, as the doors slide shut behind us. The coast is clear, and luckily there's a window in the room. I run over to open it, but Teal looks at me strangely and shows me that it's just a computer screen of a beautiful landscape scene embedded in the wall. I shrug sheepishly and follow him to an air duct opening near the ceiling, covered by a screen. We pry it off, so it dangles on its hinges. I let Teal go first, and although it's a tight fit, I manage to climb through. Pulling the cover back on, I crawl on all fours to catch up.

"Hey, where would they take blue prisoners?" I send Teal the thought. "I need to find my friends."

"I know where. Is no safe for us. Chief TopMost chamber," he answers.

I don't hesitate. "Can you take me there?"

We crawl through the air duct system of the alien megastructure. "What planet is this?" I ESP.

"Ka'Azula is our world. Mean 'Great Blue,'" he replies proudly.

"Is that why they only like blue people? Like them?" I am shocked and saddened by this situation, but I know it happens on our planet too. "Is that why they call us toxic? Because we don't have blue skin?" I ask, clenching my teeth as I struggle through the grey tunnel. I think of the time my pop got pulled over by the police for no reason. They just wanted to make sure the car he was driving wasn't stolen. He told me not to worry, that this happens sometimes. But I could tell he was worried and scared. He reminded me always to be polite with the police and never run away from them.

Teal is talking, pulling me out of my thoughts about Pop. "Is AIN Law of Sameness. In Ka'Azula, if live thirteen Kas must take sameness capsule for cells of beauty-blue. Most admired and desired cell color in all Ka'Azula. Shaman say this pleases AIN." Teal hangs his head down, "Me still Red. AIN no happy, have failed my thirteen Ka passage!" He slows down and starts to cry. "Have toxic cells. Soon, taken from family to go to red colony forever."

"Where's that?" I ask in disbelief at this racist rule. I struggle behind him in the small shaft.

"Far, far away. No give toxic cell disease to others," Teal snivels, resigned to his fate, he starts crawling again.

"But red skin isn't a disease," I try to console him. "Just like my tan skin isn't a disease or poison. This is racism or . . . or . . . colorism or something. How can they treat beings badly because of how they look on

the outside. Who is this AIN guy, anyway?" I exclaim, trying to keep up with Teal.

"AIN is great spirit in sky, watching all. AIN love beauty-blue." Teal slows down as he explains, "Want Ka'Azula to be good . . . to be blue. Red bad, red toxic!" Teal sobs and wipes his huge eyes with his tattered sleeve.

"Our skin is not toxic or bad. Let's find my friends, and we'll all help you," I promise as Teal suddenly disappears from my view. I hear him squawking as he falls through a loose grate. "What the . . ." I scramble forward and see nothing but Teal's back claws clinging desperately to the edge of the gaping hole. I pull him back into the tunnel by his legs, glad that he is still holding onto the grate. He pulls it back up with him. He looks at me with gratitude as his little beak opens and closes. "We're a good team, little buddy," I say, patting him on the shoulder. We are both panting and sweating with our close call and almost being discovered, but we move on.

CHAPTER 9

IT'S GOOD TO BE BLUE

"This way, think Teal," he says, turning right at the next intersection.

We hear talking and . . . wait! Is that laughter I hear coming from the air duct up ahead? We quietly approach and hear, "I wish Matt were here for this!"

"Yeah, that would make it perfect!"

It's Hawk and Celeste, and they're not being tortured or anything! It looks like they're having a . . . a . . . party!

I peer through the grate and see 'blue' Hawk and 'blue' Celeste with their feet up, being pampered by four aliens. They are sitting in big comfy chairs; two blue aliens are rubbing their feet, another one is fixing their hair, and one alien is feeding them blue grapes.

Teal and I are afraid to enter with the blue guys there, so we wait for them to finish and leave.

"Hawk, Celeste! Up here," I call from the air duct.

"What the . . . ?" Hawk looks up and spots us through the grate. "Matt! Thank god you found us. We were worried that we'd never see you again!" he exclaims, his blue face smiling as he approaches the vent.

"Come help us out of here," I say, trying to keep my voice down.

"Us? Who's us?" Celeste asks, pulling the grate off the opening and backing away as she sees Teal come out first.

"It's okay, Celeste. This is Teal. He's helping me. Teal, I want you to meet two more Earthlings, Celeste and Hawk," I ESP to him.

"Hi, Teal!" they say simultaneously.

Since they don't understand each other, I translate.

Teal stares at 'blue' Celeste with big, adoring eyes. "Earthlings blue too? So beauty-blue and red mane!" he says, reaching out to touch her long red hair. "Teal love Celeste."

"Oh . . . um, that's nice, Teal; I like you too," she says, blushing so hard she turns purple.

"Hey, are you guys having a party in here?" I ask, looking around. I guess this is how the blue side lives—soft chairs, video games, and good food!

"This is an amazing planet, Matt! They're so nice . . . and they're treating us like kings . . . er and queens." Hawk says, looking at Celeste, who is being led over to the videogame station by Teal so they can play. Squeezing in next to her on the lounge chair, he beams over at me and doesn't notice Celeste desperately trying to maintain her personal space.

"I'm not so sure, Hawk," I tell him. "They threw me in jail with nothing but a pile of dirty blankets, and Teal was hiding under them, terrified. Hawk, he's just a kid, like us. Even younger! Teal said they're going to take him from his family just because he has red skin. AND they were going to feed us worms!"

"Whoa, that's not cool!" cries Hawk, slapping his deep blue forehead. "What can we do?"

"I don't know. But Teal and I are on the run now because of the color of our skin. We have to get out of here!" I tell him.

"Okay, Matt, but let's wait for the pizza to come. I told them how to make it!" Hawk says. "And their video games are amazing! You actually go into the game!"

"What do you mean 'you go into' the game?" I ask.

"I mean, you're part of it. You experience the game first-hand. It's so awesome. There's nothing like it on Earth," he says, walking towards Celeste and Teal, who are laughing together. Suddenly, Teal and Celeste vanish before our eyes. Hawk and I look at each other.

"Huh? What just happened?" I ask him.

"They must have gone into the game," says Hawk, running over to the empty chair. "Matt, we'd better go after them! They can get into trouble all alone in there. Sit down, and hold on tight." Hawk jumps into the seat next to me and puts his hand into the palm recognition slot. "Greetings, Hawk. Do you submit to the terms of the game?" says a computerized voice.

"Yes," answers Hawk without thinking twice.

"That's weird. I didn't know computers could ESP," I say.

"Guess we can understand the underlying computer code; that's ESP with a byte," jokes Hawk.

"But . . . what are the terms?" I say too late, as I feel myself start to shrink. "W-w-w-what's h-h-h-h-happening?" The air is squeezed from my lungs, and I can hardly speak; then, we are sucked into the game.

CHAPTER 10

VIDEOGAMES GIVE US THE BLUES

Feeling disoriented, I gasp for air and look around for any sign of Celeste and Teal. No such luck. There's nothing to see except a giant map dotted with different images floating above our heads. I reach out to touch it, but Hawk roughly pulls my arm down. "Be careful what you touch. It will start a game."

We look up at a menu of choices. "What would Celeste choose?" I ask him. "What about this one?" I point to a hologram of a hamster-like animal with long fangs. "Or not . . . how about this one?" I ask, pointing to an orange orb spinning in space.

"No way, that game is way too wild. You would puke for sure!" says Hawk shaking his blue head. "Oh, here it is," he says excitedly. "This is the one we did before; she liked it. I bet she went in there with Teal." He points up at a hologram of a long 3-D snake with three heads at one end and two at the other.

"I don't know, Hawk. I think Celeste is afraid of snakes," I say, reluctant to go in myself.

"That's not a snake. It's a go-cart track, you bone-head. Let's go!" Hawk touches the map, and instantly everything changes. The scene is a super bright, outdoor setting with a track and hovering space carts appear before us. My mind is blown by what is happening. Hawk charges ahead and climbs into the

driver's seat of one of the carts, so I ride shotgun next to him. And I mean shotgun as there's a laser gun in front of me.

"Yippee-Ki-Yay!" we shout like *Star Trekkers* in space. We don't even look for seat belts as Hawk puts the pedal to the metal, and we take off down the track, from zero to a hundred in two seconds. We zig-zag along the snake-like path as I ask, "So this is a game, right?" My knuckles turn white on the dashboard. "We can't really crash into anything, right?"

I sneak a peek at Hawk, who is focused on the view ahead. "I haven't crashed into anything yet!" he answers, not making me feel better. He pulls a hairpin curve so fast that we start to skid and fish-tail along, barely hanging onto the road. Hawk gains control of the cart, and we fly over hills, avoid blockades and end with a 360-degree spin on the track. Hawk pulls back on the brake, and we surge forward right up to the checkpoint. Whew, I can breathe again. Another map appears in front of us, blocking our path. I release my death grip on the handlebar to rub my neck.

"Greetings, Hawk. Welcome to Ka level two. Solve this riddle to continue: I am light as a feather, yet the strongest being cannot hold me for more than fifty Kas?" A Ka timer starts to tick down at an alarming rate. I look over at Hawk expectantly. "What happens if we don't know the answer?"

"We have to start over. Come on, Matt, we have to catch up with Celeste. Let's think about this. What's the answer?" he grips the throttle, anxious to get going again.

"I don't know. What can't you hold for more than fifty Kas, whatever that is?" I repeat, wracking my brain for the answer. Suddenly, a light bulb goes on in my head, "I got it. It's your breath! It weighs nothing, but you can't hold it for long." I scream at the map, "Breath! Breath!" The timer stops with two Kas to go.

"Congratulations, Hawk! You've made it to . . ." Hawk pushes down on the throttle, and we are off again on our wild ride down the track, except this time, targets are popping up along the way.

"Quick, Matt! You have to shoot at the red aliens with that ray gun in front of you. NOW!" he yells as a target with a red being pops up.

"Shoot it!" he yells again, rounding a curve. I grab the ray gun, take aim and pull the trigger; *Pew, Pew*! Bullseye. The next target is a blue being. "Don't shoot the blue ones, only the reds!" Hawk tells me as we zoom through a cartoon desert scape with pink sand, purple cacti, and a big glittery-green sky. The targets continue to pop up along the way as I try my best to shoot down every red alien I see. *Pew, Pew*! I notice that the red alien targets are doing evil things like stealing food and killing. While the blue targets are smelling flowers, smiling, or giving a Ka salute. *Pew, Pew!*

I try not to think about the game's obvious dis-crimination against red beings. My pop told me that discrimination is a hidden thing. It's not always about calling you names; sometimes, it's when they don't call your name, and you know it's because they don't trust you or want you.

Our score keeps going up as I rake in the points. *Pew, pew!* I blast away at targets to my left, to my right, down a hole, behind a cactus. I feel a surge of guilt and wonder how Teal must feel having to shoot at every red alien target. Hawk rockets us down the track, miraculously avoiding crashing into anything.

"Where did you learn to drive like this?" I ask without looking at him. Bam! I take a shot at a red alien choking a small animal as we abruptly stop at another checkpoint.

"Greetings, Hawk. Welcome to Ka level three. Solve this riddle to continue: What is dark but made by light?" Once again, the Ka timer starts to tick down, waiting for our answer.

I can see why Celeste likes this game. It's a brain-buster!

"Matt, hurry, what's the answer?" says Hawk, pushing on the throttle, revving it impatiently.

"I don't know! Think, think! What is dark but made by light?" I look around desperately as the Kas run out. Hawk repeats the riddle as I notice something on the ground next to us. "Our shadow!" I yell, "A shadow is dark but made by light!" Just in time to stop the Ka timer! "Phew!"

"Congratulations, Hawk! You've made it to . . ." Hawk pushes down hard on the petal, and we fly off on our quest to catch up to Celeste and Teal and, hopefully, find an exit. I want to get out of this rat race. "Wow, Matt, you're the riddle master," Hawk says, looking sideways at me in total amazement.

Everything suddenly goes dark in the game, like we're in outer space. It's hard to tell if we're driving or flying or even how fast we're going. There's no sky or path ahead of us, and it's hard to orient ourselves.

"I never made it to this level before, Matt," says Hawk. As we silently make our way to the next checkpoint, we search around the eerie blackness for targets or anything that may jump out at us.

CHAPTER 11

GAME ON

I notice a video screen between Hawk and me in the cart, so I turn it on. It shows the room we'd just left, and I see the blue guys looking for us. "Uuuh, Hawk, looks like we have trouble," I say, pointing at the screen.

"Here, push down on this button, and we'll be able to hear them. It's an intercom." He explains as we suddenly hear them arguing.

"I ordered you to watch over the Earthlings." says the Chief coolly to his guards, narrowing his enormous eyes to menacing little slits. "What do you fools have to say for yourselves?"

"But, but Chief TopMost, we were trying to get information from them in exchange for something called pizza," whines a bluish-faced guard.

"You had better find them, Aqua, or I'll revoke your blue status and downgrade you to turquoise!" Chief TopMost utters, with a sneer of his prominent blue beak, his small horns pointing accusingly.

"No! Please, Chief, anything but that!" Aqua pleads, throwing himself on the ground at the Chief's feet. "Some of my greenish ancestors were sent to the 'Green Colony' and, and they suffered unspeakable horrors." He sniffles and rubs his runny beak on his sleeve. "I-I-I think they are inside the games! We will help locate them and recommend you send Bluest-One in to retrieve them," he cries and grabs onto TopMost's leg burying his face.

"Yes, alright, if anyone can catch up with them in the games, it is my son," Chief TopMost says proudly. "Move it, now! We cannot allow them to get to the final Ka level! I will recall Bluest-One from Azulazone immediately for the mission." Chief TopMost pulls his back leg from Aqua's grasp and almost trips as he leaves the room.

"Uh-oh!" I say, switching off the intercom. We watch Aqua and the other guard walk towards the video game station. "Let's find Celeste and get out of here," I say as we are suddenly blasted by another space cart rocketing toward us. We go spinning out-of-control, into the black void of space. The back of our cart catches fire, and I use the laser gun to blast off the burning part.

"What the heck was that? Hawk, we're under attack!" I yell as Hawk tries to right our space cart with the controls.

"I should have told you sooner, but every level gets more and more challenging," says Hawk, shaking his blue-blond hair to clear his head. "I guess we're the target now!"

"Let's get out of here, Hawk. It looks like there's another cart coming at us!" I warn him as I tighten my seat belt to brace for another hit.

"Get your gun ready, Matt! We're not going down without a fight," Hawk cries as he roars our space cart up out of the deep void and charges the other space cart head-on. I grab the ray gun and take careful aim as our two space carts hurl towards each other in a wild game of space-chicken.

"Yippee Ki-Yay!" I scream like the 'Star Trekkers' when they're about to conquer the enemy aliens. *Pew, pew*! I pull the trigger and just miss the mark as the other space cart quickly drops below us, out of sight. *Pew, pew!* We hear them firing at us from behind. Hawk flies serpentine, like we did on planetoid Shnergla, to avoid the attack of the laser drones. "This is awesome, Hawk!" I cry as we out-maneuver them, and Hawk goes full throttle, leaving them in our space-dust.

"That was way cool, partner," he says, rocketing through the darkness and high-fiving me at the same time.

"Yeah, but keep your hands on the wheel, Hawk. I think I see another cart up ahead! Get ready!" I say, wiping my sweaty hands on my pants and clenching my gun. "They're trying to trick us by hovering low over there. They'll probably spring an attack on us any moment. Let's fly over them and flush them out!"

"Yippee Ki-Yay!" I scream again as we zoom over to the enemy's location. I aim the ray gun and slowly pull on the trigger, hoping to blast *them* into oblivion this time.

Suddenly Hawk screams, "Don't shoot!" I immediately aim the ray gun up and fire a couple of lasers into the empty space above us as I notice Celeste and Teal waving frantically at us from the other cart.

CHAPTER 12

WHO'S THE BLUEST OF THEM ALL?

"**C**eleste, Teal! Are you okay?" I call over to them as Hawk glides down alongside them. I can see Celeste has been crying blue tears.

"Y-y-yes, we're okay, now," Celeste says, sniffling and holding up Teal's tiny, clawed hand. "But it's been pretty scary! They're trying to take us out."

"I know! This game is a simulated reality, like the *Matrix* or something," I say, quickly putting my ray gun back in the holster.

"We hide many time, and Celeste has wise puzzle brain." ESPs Teal, looking adoringly at Celeste, who smiles back at him.

"Why don't you guys climb in here with us, and let's get to the next checkpoint," Hawk says.

"I thought you'd never ask," says Celeste pushing Teal towards our cart and climbing in after him. They squeeze into the back, "Thanks for coming to our rescue, guys," she says, hooking a long strand of red hair behind her blue ear.

"We've been watching the blue guys on this video screen." I show Celeste. "They're planning to send someone in after us. Someone called Bluest-One."

"Bluest-One, coming to get . . . us!" squeals Teal, scrunching up his beak and throwing his short arms up over his head. "He most beauty-blue in all Ka'Azula!

Every being love!" He is so excited that he starts to splutter and hyperventilate. Holding his bird-like chest to calm down, he says something none of us wants to hear, "Bluest-One worthy in all things . . . most worthy in matrix games."

"Let's blast off, bud!" I say to Hawk, feeling like our game just changed to 'Cat and Mouse.' And we're the mouse.

We go into stealth mode, moving from one hiding spot to another until we reach the next checkpoint. The game is a lot eerier now, as we hover low to avoid bumping into anything when something occurs to me.

"Hey, I just remembered something Chief TopMost said to his guards. He told them not to let us get to the final Ka level. I wonder what he meant by that?" I ask everyone.

"Well, there are five levels in this game, so two more levels, and we'll find out. But we have to get there first," says Celeste.

We see the checkpoint in the distance when suddenly everything starts to disappear as a thick fog emerges from nowhere. It's like the smoke machine we had for the Halloween party at school last year. It was very cool then, not so much now.

"Oh man, they're coming after us, Matt!" says Hawk, speeding up in the direction of the checkpoint. "This is a fog bomb, which is never a good thing. They're trying to blind us," he warns. Hawk slows down again because we can't see anything in front of us. Waves of fog roll in—the place looks haunted, and it smells of rotten eggs. "Ewwww smells like sulfur," he says.

"Yeah, this is creepy and stinky," I say, holding my nose and trying to adapt to the low visibility. "Go to da right, Awk, I tink it's ober dere." I choke as I pull out my ray gun for security. I scan the foggy landscape to the left, right, and front of us. I have the feeling something monstrous will come out of the fog at any moment.

"I think I see something up ahead," Hawk tells us.

"Yes! There it is!" points Celeste from the back seat. "Go, Hawk!"

He glides down to the hidden checkpoint. We see a massive laser blast coming right at us, but it explodes just inches away like it hit a force field.

Teal wipes his brow. "Safe zone. First blast no hit us. Now we big target."

"Greetings, Hawk. Welcome to Ka level four. Solve this riddle to continue: What gets bigger the more you take away?" The Ka timer ticks down, waiting for the answer.

"I'm starting to hate riddles," groans Hawk. "Well, Riddle Master, what's the answer?" he asks.

I look over at Hawk in frustration. "Anyone got any ideas? What gets bigger the more you take away?" I ask in a rush as time is running out. Hawk and Celeste brainstorm as I look around, aiming my ray gun at the threatening fog. I see two yellow eyes bouncing in the distance, swerving in our direction.

"Hurry up, guys! What's the answer? Something's coming. Think! Think! What gets bigger the more you take away?" I keep my ray gun aimed at the approaching monster as a small voice pops up in my head, "Hole."

"That's it, Teal! That's the answer, a hole." As soon as I say the word, we are sucked into the next level, just as the monster with yellow eyes gets close enough to see that it's another space cart with yellow fog lights and an angry blue face at the wheel.

CHAPTER 13

HANG ONTO YOUR CART

"Thanks, Teal, you saved us back there." I ESP him as we hear, "Congratulations, Hawk! Welcome to K- a - l –e –v –e -l . . ." The game slows down and stops like it ran out of power. We look at each other, confused.

"I think we broke the game. That would stall the other guys from coming through," Hawk says.

When the power resumes, we are in a canyon setting, with deep valleys and gorges for miles. It's an awesome sight.

Hawk tells us, "This place makes me think of the Grand Canyon where Grandpa took me star-gazing and taught me how to identify the planets and constellations. Orion the hunter, Ursa Minor or little bear, and Ursa Major with the seven stars of the Big Dipper. He passed on his love of the universe to me. He and his radio are the reason we're here right now." I see he's getting a little choked up.

I miss my grandpoppa too, and all the time I spent on the farm where he worked. Mom said it was sad that he worked his fingers to the bone on that farm, but he couldn't pass it on to Pop because he never owned it—he was a tenant farmer who just lived on the land and worked it.

I see a big sky surrounding us in different shades

of blue, and the ground is layers of rusty reds and brownish-orange colored soils. Our space cart has become an ATV after Hawk found the button that popped out our wheels, and we're off-roading it across the dusty terrain. The ATV has big balloon tires, so we're high off the ground, and Hawk's having the time of his life bouncing over boulders. I yell out to him, "You better slow down, or you're going to break something . . . like my neck!"

Hawk replies, "Do you see the wheels on this thing? We can do anything!" There's a loud bang as he answers, and we're all bounced out of our seats. "OK, so that was too much," Hawk says, slowing down a little.

"What are we supposed to do at this level?" asks Celeste.

Teal replies, "No fall in crater. Shoot azulanimals and azulizards. Like that!" Teal points at a big orange iguanodon, camouflaged like a chameleon and running towards us. He swings his broad tail into the side of our cart as Hawk veers hard to the left to avoid him.

"Watch out, Hawk, you almost went over the edge of the canyon!" Celeste warns as Teal jumps into her lap, covering his eyes. I can see she's rubbing the worry stone that she always keeps in her pocket.

I wipe the sweat off my forehead and look out the front window of the cart when something huge lands on the windshield. Splat! "Aaaah!!" Hawk and I shriek in surprise. "What is that thing, Matt?"

"It looks like a giant, neon-pink slug. But I've never seen one this big before. It's at least a foot long!" I shudder as I see it slither across the window, leaving a trail of pink slime behind it. "It's trying to block out our view with its slime," I tell Hawk.

"Too bad we don't have any windshield wipers," Hawk says, banging on the window and veering close to the canyon's edge again.

"Careful, Hawk!" yells Celeste from the backseat.

"Uh, oh!" The slime seems to be burning a hole through the window, causing pink smoke to seep into our cart.

"Matt, you better get him off of there, or he's going to be in here soon with his slimy acid!" yells Hawk, jerking the steering wheel to avoid the canyon's edge.

I reach outside the cart with my ray gun and try to shoot the slug off the window. *Pew, pew*! I miss him the first time but slice him in half with the second shot, and he flies off the window in two pieces.

"Nice shootin', partner," yells Hawk, laughing. "Hey, Teal, just curious, what happens if they knock us into the canyon?"

"Teal think, the end," he replies.

I'm not sure if he means the end of the game or the end of us.

We notice a couple of warthogs with spikes around their necks and curly tails like scorpions running alongside us. Suddenly there's a whole herd of them, forcing us off the road! *Pew, pew!* I try to scare them away from our cart. "Go faster, Hawk! These roadhogs are strong, trying to push us off the edge."

Hawk speeds up and takes a hard left over a large boulder. We almost tip over as our cart tilts to the left and the road curves to the right. We hang off the edge for a few seconds before the ATV rights itself.

"Wow, that was a close one." Hawk's blue face almost turns back to white!

CHAPTER 14

WHO'S ON THE EDGE?

Teal looks out the back of the cart, excitedly pointing. "There, Bluest-One!"

We see the guard, Aqua, at the wheel, and Bluest-One aims his ray gun in our direction.

"Go, Hawk!" I yell, and he goes full throttle, blasting orange sand everywhere as the balloon tires spin in place before grabbing. We zoom out in front but then they roar up alongside our cart. "Get down!" I shout at Celeste and Teal when I hear Aqua bark, "Shoot the red mutant, and the game will end. Do not hit the others—TopMost wants them alive."

"I know my mission, and I never miss a red target." Bluest-One replies. His nubby horns point at us as he aims his ray gun at our back seat. He misses his shot as Hawk cuts in front of them, forcing them back. Bluest-One's beak twitches angrily.

I hear Teal's little voice in my head. "If Bluest-One shoot me, game end, you safe." I look in the back to see him edge toward the door of the cart as Celeste tries to hold him back. "I jump, you go fast, he no stop you," he says.

"No Teal, don't do this!" cries Celeste as she pulls him back into his seat. "Now he'll have to risk shooting me."

"Teal no want you suffer. Earthlings must go back home," he tells Celeste as she pulls him down to shelter him with her body. *Pew, pew!*

"He's aiming for you, Celeste. Get down!" I shout as their ATV closes the distance between us again, and Bluest-One aims his ray gun at Teal. He takes a shot; *Pew, pew!* Just as an azulizard leaps from a rock towards our cart. Zap! The giant alien lizard is blown apart by the laser. The blast saves Celeste and Teal from the creature, and the azulizard strike spares them from the laser. Hawk speeds up, driving serpentine to make it harder for Bluest-One to shoot at us.

"Good driving, Hawk! But watch out for the edge! Aaaah!" I scream as he swerves dangerously close to the rim.

"I go now!" ESPs Teal urgently, as a laser whizzes past their heads, *Pew*, singeing Celeste's hair. Celeste flies back in her seat as Teal jumps up, going for the door. *Pew, pew!* Bluest-One fires again, right at Teal, who is now in the open. Amazingly, the laser beam veers off to the left without causing any damage. Bluest-One looks confused and shoots again; *Pew, pew!* This time it bends harmlessly to the right, not even close to our cart. Teal is standing and staring like a frozen red deer in the headlights, but Bluest-One's blasts keep missing him. I realize Celeste is using her telekinesis to veer the lasers away from Teal.

I hear Bluest-One yell to Aqua, "Get closer. I will go up on top up front for a better shot." Aqua zooms up close again as Hawk slows down to get around the narrow rim of the canyon. Bluest-One climbs out onto the roof of their ATV just as another large, blue azulizard swings down from a dead tree.

The reptile crashes onto their cart and knocks Bluest-One to the edge of the roof.

Hawk slams on the brakes, forcing Aqua to swerve right to avoid smashing into the back of our cart. His turn causes Bluest-One to fly off to the left, into the canyon, taking the lizard with him.

Teal sees this and shouts, "Nooo, wait Bluest-One." He jumps out of the cart towards the shrieking blue alien.

Celeste watches him, focusing her power on Teal as he flies into the canyon. She directs him toward Bluest-One as the lizard whizzes past them, down into the crater. It lands with a dead thud at the bottom. Celeste struggles to elevate them as Teal, and a very surprised Bluest-One, rise slowly out of the canyon. Hawk jumps from the driver's seat and reaches out to help pull them toward the canyon's rim. Teal and Bluest-One fall to the ground, trembling with relief. We all stare, not sure what's going to happen. Bluest-One reaches out his blue talon to Teal and pats him on the back. We all breathe a sigh of relief and run to them.

"Thanks for saving me!" Bluest-One says, looking up at all of us, "even though I was trying to shoot you. Earthlings have special powers." He hangs his head then looks over at Teal. "What's your name?"

"Me Teal." He replies shyly.

"Why did you help me?" Bluest-One asks.

"Me no want you die, like azulizard." We all look down at the lifeless blue body at the bottom of the canyon.

"I guess we have something in common." says Bluest-One.

Aqua runs over to Bluest-One, "Oh, it's my fault. Thank you for not dying, Bluest-One! Your father would have down-graded me for sure!" he cries.

"I am happy you won't have to face that, but you have them to thank for it." Bluest-One nods at us.

"High-five, little dude!" I say, holding my hand up in front of Teal, who looks at me and raises a tentative talon to tap my hand.

He then turns to Bluest-One and holds up his red talon for a high-three.

Suddenly, we hear a voice over the intercom, "All players proceed to Ka level five. Repeat - proceed to Ka level five."

"What? We have to continue this dangerous game of hunter and prey?" Hawk asks, looking at everyone. "Someone almost died!"

"Yes, we must," explains Aqua. "Chief TopMost designed the game, and we must get to the end. But I am afraid red beings cannot leave level 5."

I look over at Teal's red face—he's trembling.

"But, but that means Teal could die! That's, that's not right!" Celeste cries in disbelief.

"If we can win Ka level five, we will be safe, and I have an idea of how we can fool the game. If so, Teal will be a free being, able to live as he pleases," Bluest-One adds.

"What happens if we don't win?" I ask.

"Teal will have to stay inside the game as a target," Aqua replies sadly. We all look at Teal, who twitches his little beak and wipes a tear from his eye. "Teal want be free," he murmurs. "Live with family, forever."

"There's only one thing to do then. We have to win the last level and trick the game," I say, looking around at the others. We make a circle around Teal and high-five together, chanting 'Real-Teal' over his head, holding claw to hand, then head for our carts and our destiny.

CHAPTER 15

STAYING ALIVE

"Hello, Hawk. Welcome to Ka level five. Solve this riddle to continue: What is always in front of you, but cannot be seen?" Both carts are working together to figure out the riddle at the checkpoint.

Six heads are better than two. *Right!*

"Come on, guys, what's always in front of you, but you can't see it?" I tell everyone to think of something.

"How about your nose?" Hawk asks, crossing his eyes to look at his nose. Nothing happens; Kas tick down.

"What about the road?" Celeste says. Nothing happens.

"Maybe air?" Aqua shrugs. Nothing happens. Kas keep ticking down.

"I know! It's ahead. Get it, a – head, haha?" I try with a laugh. Celeste and Hawk look at each other and roll their eyes as nothing happens. Kas are running out.

Having played this game before, Bluest-One says, "It is the future, of course."

"Ahh, right!" I say, and we all high-five each other.

"Welcome to Ka level five," we hear behind us. Both carts take off like a race, only to stop abruptly. We find ourselves in a room where our ATVs disappear from under us, and we're left standing there together. *Wait! What?*

"Oh, cool," says Celeste, looking around. "I've heard about these games. It's an 'Escape Room.' You have to work together and find the clues to set you free," she says, starting to search around. She points out a timer on the wall showing the Kas ticking down from 300.

"Let's look around for clues, everyone. We don't have much time," Hawks calls out. We notice details in the alien workstation: a desk, some cabinets and boxes against a wall, computer screens displaying hieroglyphs, and a control module dominating the middle of the room.

"Bluest-One, have you escaped from this room before?" Hawk asks him hopefully as he explores the command center.

"No, it was a different chamber, and I was not successful," he answers, opening boxes. "But I found a clue," he says, holding up a crystal.

"If you find anything, bring it over to the desk so we can figure out the answer," Hawk tells everyone as we search the room.

Aqua holds something up. "I found a microchip."

Celeste responds, "Maybe it goes in these slots over here in the control module."

"Looks like we're getting somewhere," I say as the Kas tick down to 150.

Hawk and I stare at the screen of hieroglyphic symbols, but it's all alien to us. It shows; soaring birds, an eyeball, a talon, a moon, a key, and a picture of 6 stick figures (four blue, one red, and one tan).

"Teal, do you know what this means?" I ESP him, and he runs over to us. He studies the symbols and decodes. "Freedom seen when you walk beyond locked moon."

"Wow, it says all that?" I say as I look at him in admiration. "Come over here, everyone. Teal cracked the code!"

Teal repeats his message as we look at the other clues we found. Hawk leans on the wall, activating a hologram. It's a moon with a door beside it on the opposite wall. "Hey, guys! Look what I can do," he says, pushing against the wall again to make the image disappear and reappear. "This is what we were looking for—a door beside the moon."

"Nice going, Hawk!" I say, high-fiving him.

"OK, everyone, let's plug in the other clues to see if it will open the door," Hawk says.

"Hurry, we only have 50 Kas left," warns Celeste.

"OK, microchip," Hawk says, pointing to Aqua, who inserts the microchip into the slot, lighting up a keyhole on the door.

"Now crystal," Hawk says, pointing to Bluest-One, who places the blue crystal into the keyhole. The door spins to an open position, and six round spots appear on the floor in front of it.

Hawk yells, "Yippee Ki-Yay! Jump on the spots, everybody."

"Wait!" cries Teal. "Must match."

Celeste nods, "He's right, tan for Matt and red for Teal."

We all claim our spots, but Teal's disappears as he jumps on it.

One by one, we are teleported through the gateway,

like we are melting. Bluest-One, who is on the last blue spot, grabs Teal at the last second, not wanting to leave him behind.

We fly through a portal on a collision course with the moon. Sparks fly everywhere as we slide down a chute and land in the room where the game started. "Congratulations, Ka level five completed!" *Phew! I think it was all holographic!*

Celeste looks around and cries, "Where's Teal? Did he make it?"

"Yes," replies Bluest-One, "He is here, with me."

We all look over at Bluest-One, holding a beaming Teal, and they are both purple. It's as though some of Bluest-One's color has leaked onto Teal and Teal's color onto Bluest-One.

CHAPTER 16

THE ABYSS

We run over to Bluest-One and Teal, laughing and high-fiving each other. We don't hear the door open or Chief TopMost entering the room. He stands watching us before speaking. "Hello, my son," he says, startling us all into silence.

"Father, the Earthlings are friends . . ." Bluest-One starts to say when TopMost interrupts him.

"Seize the invaders and take them to the dungeon chamber," barks Chief TopMost. "Bring Bluest-One to my private chamber, now!" He looks at his son, pointing his menacing little horns in his direction. The blue guards march toward us and roughly lead us out of the game room.

"But we won the game!" Hawk says, pulling away. "This isn't fair!"

"We're not eating any worms!" I cry, searching for Teal, who they are tying up with ropes. "Wait, what are you doing to Teal?"

"We don't want him using his magical charms to escape," TopMost says, as he leaves the room. ". . . or help you to escape."

"But Father, you don't understand," Bluest-One protests as he is dragged away from us.

The chief pauses, turns around and says, "I understand that my guards are injured, our structural duct system is contaminated by toxic cell disease, and our matrix games have been hacked and infected with a matrix virus. Even my son is poisoned. All because of these . . . these outsiders. They do not belong here, and we must dispose of them. Just as we dispose of bluish-green guards who disobey their orders." He finishes with a flourish then turns to follow Bluest-One. There's a sudden shrieking from behind us, "Nooooo . . ."

We turn as Aqua shoots out of the matrix chamber and hits Chief TopMost in the chest, knocking him off balance. His arms go out to steady himself, but he's close to the edge of the walkway and starts to fall. The chief reflexively pinwheels his arms in wide circles and kicks out a talon. But it's no use; he starts to go over the edge. I flick my eyes beyond him and see a black void leading to a bottomless pit.

The alien megastructure is designed like a donut—with a hole in the middle—the abyss TopMost is tumbling down.

"Father!" cries Bluest-One as Teal takes action. Levitating above our heads, he soars toward Chief TopMost to grab his claw just in time. The dazed guards use the rope they're still holding to reel them both in. Hawk and I look over at Celeste, and she shakes her head and puts her hands palm up to show that she is not using her levitation superpowers this time. We are all blown away that Teal must be doing this himself! Some of Celeste's power must have transferred to the one who needed it here—Teal.

Bluest-One approaches his father and Teal, who sit together on the floor, smiling at each other. "See, Father, they are our friends."

Aqua runs over to the group. "Chief TopMost, thank you for not falling into the bottomless abyss. I would never have forgiven myself if you'd disappeared into the black void of death. I do not know what happened. A force suddenly pushed me in your direction. Like a wind or suction . . . I did not mean for this to happen! Waaaah! I did not mean it!" Aqua throws himself at the mercy of the Chief, crying and sniffling on his leg again.

Chief TopMost rolls his eyes, "Get off me, Aqua. I believe you. Many strange things are happening to us right now, and my eyes are open to a great wrong in our society. Let us go into the confer chamber to discuss our future."

CHAPTER 17

THE COLOR PURPLE

We follow Bluest-One into a grand meeting room that looks like a capsule floating in outer space. "This is so cool!" I look around as Hawk, and I high-five. The clear glass windshields are curved outwards to refract light and create an inter-cosmic, optical illusion. Billions of stars light up the dark sky, and a giant eye looks back at us from deep space. I stumble back from the view, "Whoa! Who's watching us?" I ask Bluest-One, and he chuckles at my reaction.

"That is 'AIN,' the Eye of the spirit. Our Shaman tells us that AIN watches over us and cries tears because we are not enlightened, and he begs for us to become."

"Oh, thanks. That explains everything . . . Wait, become what?" I ask, eyeing the Eye warily.

"Shaman says we will know when we are," replies Bluest-One.

"Are what?!" I implore, holding my head as I try to get my mind around this complex idea. "Help me out here, Hawk." Bluest-One and Hawk shrug their shoulders as we sit down on bouncy chairs and wait for Chief TopMost to join us.

When TopMost enters, he has an ice pack perched on his head, looking down at his tablet. Aqua is trailing behind him. When he finally looks around, he seems sad, especially as the melting ice pack slides to the side of his head. "I have an apology to make to our guests from Earth." He looks away, searching for words he has never used before. "I was not a gracious host, and I hope to make up for that. I also want to apologize to Bluest-One and Teal. Seeing you come through the portal the same color made me very angry. I sensed that our system of rules and laws was breaking down, and I was afraid."

"I understand, Father. I felt the same way as my mission in the matrix games progressed," Bluest-One says, looking over at Teal.

Chief TopMost nods at his son, "When I saw how you all worked together in the games and that beings of different outer shell color could get along, I was troubled. The truth is, I did not want to allow beings of other colors the same respect as blue beings."

"But they saved my life at the canyon," Bluest-One interrupts.

"Yes, and for that, I am grateful. I didn't expect you to be in danger, and I was wrong to put red beings in our Matrix games for sport," Chief TopMost looks around at us. His gaze rests on Celeste, whose skin is fading to light blue, "Blue face and red mane, Celeste, you show me the beauty of both colors. I would like to hear from you." he says.

She looks down, and I can see she is rubbing the worry stone in her pocket. "You can learn a lot from your son. He is beautiful on the inside, but he tried to please you by hating beings with other skin colors. Teal showed him what unconditional love is," she says quietly, casting a glance at Bluest-One.

TopMost hangs his head, nodding, "I am learning too—from both of them."

He shifts his gaze to Hawk, "Hawk, you have proven yourself a worthy game master. Can you share some of your knowledge with me?"

"First of all, your video games are awesome!" He turns and high-fives me. "But players and targets shouldn't really die in them! That's not fun," Hawk says, getting serious.

TopMost taps on his tablet and continues around the circle, "Matt, the Riddle Master, you avoided our sameness capsule and escaped our dungeon chamber. You accepted Teal and became his friend. That helped you win the matrix games and taught me a lesson. I want to thank you."

"I learned what it feels like to be treated like a lesser being because of my skin color. It's not a good feeling. Now I know what my pop and his family have to go through in our world, just because they have dark skin. I will never feel guilty about my skin color or be ashamed of my family, brown or white, because that's what makes me, *Me.* I have learned something else; beings should be accepted because they're kind, like Aqua, and amazing like Teal. Maybe then your great spirit in the sky would be happy." I beam at Bluest-One as I share my insight. My bouncy chair starts to roll backward, and I slide off it with a thud.

CHAPTER 18

AIN'S LAW

Chief TopMost's head snaps up in surprise. He looks toward the window and the Eye in the sky. Somehow the AIN appears less sad. TopMost gets up and paces in front of us, muttering to himself and tapping on his tablet. Finally, he says, "You are right, Matt. AIN was unhappy with us, and we never knew why. I see now that we, on Ka'Azula, must evolve. We must change our laws and customs to unite our people—to please our watchful 'Eye' in the sky."

"Father, I hope you will accept Teal and me as beings of a new and beautiful Ka'Azulian outer shell color—Bluest-Grape." Bluest-One continues, "When Teal and I transited the passage together, our colors merged." He puts up a talon to high-three Teal. "My little brother has changed not only my color but also my thinking and feeling," Bluest-One says solemnly.

"Yes, Bluest-One. It is clear that beings of other colors are smart, compassionate, and loyal" TopMost continued, "I now see how things can be . . . different on Ka'Azula. I want to declare an end to our 'Sameness' passage and embrace our 'Otherness.'"

"Red not toxic?" asks Teal.

"That's right. As of this day, we are one race of multi-colors. Ka'Azulians." Everyone at the table jumps up, clapping and smiling at each other. The cosmic Eye in the starry dark sky is twinkling back at us.

Chief TopMost reaches out his blue talon to Teal, who grasps the offered claw. "Teal, I want you to study with the High-Shaman and help to make peace with AIN. You are not only intelligent but gifted with mystical strength and power of mind," he says to the tiny purple being in front of him. "I regret that we did not recognize these gifts sooner. You will be reunited with your family, and when you are ready, you will start your apprenticeship."

Teal wipes a tear off his purple face with his tattered sleeve and snorts loudly, "Teal knows not what say."

I tell him, "Hey, little dude. I'm glad you're going home. I knew we could do it. Like my mom always says: we can do whatever we set our minds to!"

"Matt ma'ams very wise, think Teal," he sniffs, his big eyes full of tears. "Teal want see his ma'ams too. She teach, be nice to others, so they nice also."

"I guess moms can be pretty smart. I'll try that with Big Mikey," I say.

Aqua pipes up, "Ahem! I have an announcement to make. The galley chamber has been working to create eats for the Earthlings, and I am proud to say that we will partake of our first 'pizza' together. Follow me, everyone." Our noses follow the wonderful aroma of freshly baked bread and creamy cheese.

"Woohoo! Pizza-party!" I high-five everyone. "Then, can we play another video game?" I joke.

Celeste looks at Hawk and groans. "No way, Matt! Don't even joke about that," she says, rubbing her worry stone.

"Hey, Aqua!" Hawk calls, catching up to him. "Can I get some cola and milk from the galley kitchen?"

Aqua stops and turns to face us. His curved, greenish-blue nose wriggles, and his bird-like tongue darts from side to side, "Eech! You Earthlings consume strange things!"

I know you're wondering how the Ka'pizza tasted. It was the most amazing pizza we've ever had. It covered the whole table, at least 10 feet across, and it was delicious, full of saucy sauce, cheesy cheese, and some kind of blue sausage on top. I didn't ask, but I think it was azulizard-sausage.

HAWK'S EPILOGUE

And I think it's gonna be a long, long time.
'Till touchdown brings me round again to find.
I'm not the boy they think I am at all. Oh no, no,
no. I'm a rocket boy... rocket boy...rocket boy...
—Based on "Rocketman." Music by Elton John,
lyrics by Bernie Taupin

"Hawk!" Huh! I wake up to my mom's voice. I've been dreaming! Here, on our sofa in 'Mission Control.' I see Matt and Celeste are still asleep with saucy sauce on their faces. I am relieved that we are all back to our normal skin colors. Wow, did we really just have a pizza party with some cool aliens on planet Ka'Azula? I remember eating so much pizza, watching a re-play of our video game, and laughing so much we almost puked. Then it was time to say good-bye. Teal cried as he gave us all a big hug and wished us a safe journey. He ESPed to me, 'Tell Celeste thank you.' I looked at him in surprise, then remembered how clever he is. They led us back to the wormhole, and . . . whoosh! The best pizza dreams ever. Before we left, we saw the cosmic Eye galaxy glowing in a rainbow of colors. But I'm happy to be back in our own galaxy, sliding into home on the Milky Way. "Coming, Mom," I answer.

AUTHOR'S NOTE

Bill of Rights for Mixed Race Children
by Sara-Momii Roberts, 2021
(https://www.embracerace.org)

- I have the right not to be bullied for who I am
- I have the right to be what I say I am
- I have the right not to be teased about who I am
- I have the right to call myself what I want to call myself
- I have the right to be friends with whoever I want
- I have the right to look different than my sisters or brothers, and that's ok

GLOSSARY OF SPACE AND SCIENCE TERMS

Colorism: Discrimination based on skin color, in which beings are treated differently because of the color of their skin.

Constellation: A group of stars that form an imaginary outline or pattern, typically representing an animal, mythological god, person or creature, or other.

Discrimination: When a person or group of people is treated unfairly compared to others because of how they look, dress or act.

Drone: A flying robot that can be remotely controlled.

ESP: Extra Sensory Perception. The ability to read each other's thoughts.

Hawking, Stephen: A 20-21st century cosmologist and theoretical physicist known for his work with black holes and relativity.

Hyperspace Highway: A fictional extra-dimension of space through which starships can travel faster across the galaxy.

Intergalactic: Term meaning between galaxies.

Intuition: The ability to know or understand something without being taught.

Levitation: The raising or lifting of a person or thing by supernatural means.

Light-speed: The speed at which light travels (about 1.08 billion km per hour).

Matrix: An environment that gives form to or development of something.

Megastructure: An enormous building containing modular units designed to allow a community to be self-sufficient.

Oblivion: Unable to be found or recovered.

Portal: A gateway to another world of the past, present, or future.

Racism: Hatred of a person or the belief that another person is less than human — because of skin color, language, customs, or place of birth.

Ray gun: A weapon releasing deadly or stunning rays of unknown nature.

Simulate: To look like or imitate.

Solar panels: Units used to collect renewable energy from the sun.

Syringe: A tube with a plunger attached to a needle used to inject or take fluid out from the body.

Telekinesis: The ability to move objects at a distance by mental power.

Teleport: To be transported across space and distance instantly.

Wormhole: Tunnel connecting points in space-time in such a way that the trip between the points through the wormhole takes much less time than the trip through normal space.

ACKNOWLEDGMENTS

I am grateful to the people who helped make this book a reality. First and foremost, my supportive and creative husband, Terry Coderre. He always had the solution to the plot holes. Many thanks to my astute editor, Talya Pardo, who found the plot holes. Beta-reader Jennifer Desmarais for her invaluable input in all things SFF. And a special thank you to Janel Garcia for her advice and sensitivity read for imparting a story of racism to children. My kids, who were very enthusiastic about this endeavor from the beginning. I love you: Justin, Sophie, and Kelly.

ABOUT THE AUTHOR

Ann Birdgenaw is a librarian in an elementary school and always wanted to write a book of her own. She was inspired to write this story by a strange beeping coming from a box in her garage. When COVID-19 hit Canada, and everyone was in quarantine or lockdown, she had lots of time to imagine being sucked through a wormhole to other planets and what wonderful things she might find there.

Ann lives in Montreal, Quebec, Canada, with her family and two morkies: Bilbo and Sheba.

Send Ann a message:
https://annbirdgenaw.wordpress.com/
https://www.goodreads.com/author/
show/21269547.Ann_Birdgenaw
https://www.facebook.com/
Author-Ann-Birdgenaw-109480387962145
https://www.amazon.ca/Ann-Birdgenaw/e/
B0918TCRRT/

@abirdgenaw on Twitter
@annbirdbooks on Instagram

ABOUT THE ILLUSTRATOR

E. M. Roberts is a passionate intellectual property designer and illustrator. He graduated from Dawson College, Illustration and Design program in Montreal, Quebec. Among his interests are character design, futuristic aesthetics, and sparkling water. He lives in Montreal with his wife and two children.

Visit Ellis at:
https://www.behance.net/EllisRoberts

Stay Tuned for Labyrinthia, Book 4 in the Black Hole Radio Series!

Stay tuned for another fantastic episode of *Black Hole Radio—Labyrinthia!*

Hawk, Matt, and Celeste's adventures are just beginning! They learn to control their special powers to get on the team and win the big basketball game. They are superstars! What can go wrong? Lots, when Hawk gets stuck with Big Mikey as his science buddy, he comes snooping around the clubhouse and the Black Hole Radio . . . Beep! Beep! Beep! Not again! Can the friends survive in the deep dark caves of Planet Labyrinthia? Can they avoid the taser-wielding goons and the monstrous, screeching Hellion to free the alien children enslaved in the mine? Hawk must use his Grandpa's journals to control the radio, and save them all from the belly of the beast . . . but where's Mikey! Stay tuned!

"By the final pages, readers will know that the [friends'] adventures aren't over. Everyone that picks up a copy will be eagerly waiting for the next installment in the story. Anyone that is looking for a fun and imaginative story will enjoy spending time with Hawk, Matt, Celeste, Wolfie, and the rest of their [quirky] friends."
—Entrada Book Review